I0685431

SPRING & SUMMER 2025
VOLUME 52 NUMBER 2

In Spring 2025, *Cold Mountain Review* relaunched in an open access online format hosted by ASU's Belk Library. Print formats of each issue are available through the University of North Carolina Press. For more information, including submission guidelines, please visit https://cold-mountain-review.pubpub.org/.

Cold Mountain Review is published biannually in the Department of English at Appalachian State University. Support from ASU's Office of Academic Affairs and College of Arts and Sciences enables *CMR*'s learning and publications program. The views and opinions expressed in *CMR* do not necessarily reflect those of university trustees, administration, faculty, students, or staff.

Cold Mountain Review is indexed in the MLA International Bibliography and Humanities international Complete and is a member of The Council of Literary Magazines and Presses. Typefaces used are Arno Pro and Market Deco, designed by Sam Dalzell. Typeset by codeMantra. *CMR* logo designed by Sarah McBryde.

CONTENTS

REMEMBERING R.T. SMITH

CREATIVE NONFICTION

POETRY

CONTRIBUTORS

KATHRYN KIRKPATRICK

Out There On the Margins

This issue of *Cold Mountain Review* marks the passing of one of our founders, R.T. Smith. As an editor he was best known for stewarding Washington and Lee's literary journal, *Shenandoah,* to national prominence; we remember him at ASU as an M.A. student in the early 1970s who made from scratch a publication still determined to thrive over 50 years later. We've gathered tributes here from students, colleagues, and friends. What shines through in the memories of others is R.T.'s fierce commitment to the literary arts, his own vast multi-genre talents, and his capacity for rich, enduring friendships. Always a friend to those of us at *CMR*, he will be deeply missed by many. My own memories of him come from his Rivers Coffey residency at ASU during the spring semester of 2016, when he gave an inspiring lecture on narrative poetry, and we engaged in a long interview about his life and work: see "Some Wolf in *Cold Mountain Review*" on our on-line "About" page. Thoughtful, erudite, and by turns serious and sly, R.T. said of the founding of *Cold Mountain Review*: "When we named it we were thinking about Gary Snyder [and his translations of Han-Shan's Cold Mountain Poems (1969)]. We were not thinking about the academy at all. We were thinking about outlaw work, you know? Out there on the margins of things."

Out there on the margins, a great deal happens. I was recently reminded of the founding of the experimental, interdisciplinary Black Mountain College (1933 – 1957), also in Western North Carolina, while attending the launch of the splendid new Black Mountain poetry anthology from UNC Press. Refugee artists from Nazi Germany landed at Black Mountain, and at the time of Jim Crow, the college admitted the nation's first African American students. Later, poets Charles Olson and Robert Creeley founded *The Black Mountain Review*, publishing, among many others, the Beat poet, Gary Snyder. It's not a stretch to say that inspired by Snyder himself, R.T. and his cohort at ASU in the early 1970s were channeling some of that rebellious, innovative poetic energy. May their work inspire our own at *CMR*.

We continue to celebrate our partnership with ASU's Turchin Center for the Visual Arts for our cover this issue, featuring "Grapes" by cultural icon Andy Warhol from the Turchin's permanent collection. I love the fresh, evocative simplicity of this polaroid shot: the greens of spring meet the disarray of scattered fruit. Perhaps this is how we meet our own socio-historical era, by continuing to create enduring work that both speaks and witnesses to the moment. I find in Warhol's photograph an image both hopeful and nourishing: the grapes might yet be retrieved, nothing is yet lost. We are returned now to elemental things.

This issue opens with Molly Peacock's subtle, nuanced poems from a narrator exploring her new life as a widow in all its complexity and strangeness: "'Dead'" / now seems a relative word…Pleasure doesn't deny what / used to be pleasure." Other poems in this issue take us to the thresholds of near misses, to the boundaries between species, to the borders of meaning, as in Anna Laura Reeve's "Carolina Allspice": "I'm afraid to say something too true, / afraid of the smallest lie." Finally, each time I read Dorriane Laux's "Country," my eyes fill with tears. Perhaps that will change, and one day I'll get through it dry-eyed. Right now, I don't know how.

MOLLY PEACOCK

The Bakelite Bracelet

In a window on Third Avenue

He who loved to speed-walk the avenues
would never have ceased for a bracelet
unless dragooned, almost to the point
of ripping his jacket. Bakelite bracelet,
black circles with four jade-colored panels:
I love it! And forgot about it instantly,
the display flying by like scenery.
He was so annoying to walk with—our joint
amble always turned into: me half-a-block
behind. (That's what I got for marrying
a marathon runner.) It's a relief to walk
at my own pace now that he's dead. December:
there it was, awkwardly wrapped, over-taped
as if packed for an arctic trip, the one he'd take
through ice to leave this earth.

He, who rushed past windows on avenues,
recollected the shop's exact location
with a poised sense of live occasion,
circling back to give his forgetful enthusiast
a gift of green panels with discs attached
by a subtle entwining a bit like
our elbow-entwined walking, the only way
we could coordinate our pace, the pace
that almost ripped his jacket when I stopped,
though I forgot, and it was he who bought
foreverness to crush inside the temporary,
a stay against the rush.

MOLLY PEACOCK

Pets, Love, And Death

He was horrified when people replaced
their pets too soon. He felt a pet deserved
a dignified span of rightful mourning.
(My husband didn't want to be replaced.)
He hated my friend who reserved
a new dog the day the old one died—ignoring
its eight valiant years on this earth. But what
he could not know is that mourning
for the old one goes on in the new one's presence.
In the cock of a pet's—or a person's—head.
How a dog grabs a sock—or a man a spoon.
He did not know I would feel his presence
unspoken in ordinary chat, even as his absence
now lets me thrive at another's touch. "Dead"
now seems a relative word…Pleasure doesn't deny what
used to be pleasure. The new life's presence
invites the love he feared would go too soon.

MOLLY PEACOCK

Rejection: A How-To

The rejection comes as a tiny slice
first, the verbal cut that says, you're nothing.
Once inserted, it opens a metal wing
that whirs and keeps on slicing.
I've found I can stop that whir by feeling
awful. Hurt. By not carrying on
but letting the humiliating burn
spread into every cell its hot, peeling
energy until I'm bent and kneeling,
admitting that tiny slice was really
a knife.

I see it at the center of my life
and know I've got to pull it slowly,
concentrating on each inch of relief
until it's out. As I stare, the blood flow
vaporizes, the long blade disappears.
Hurt is released *by merely feeling it!*
—till I'm angry-in-love with my "weakness,"
that poor, frail, rejectable thing: my lowness,
the slugged child I'll adore to my death,
(distaining its rejector's fungal breath.)

MOLLY PEACOCK

Solitude and Loneliness

There is a line
between solitude and loneliness,
a little line
like the center vein of a leaf,
green rivulet...
The line between humans is like this vein,
never straight.
You recognize it only when you cross it
because now you're in
the slight re-shading
of the other side.

Though I'm lonely in wavering shadow,
I can cross to be content
in the full knowledge of my pattern that
a solitary being has.
Solitude? A present to myself.
Loneliness?
The absence of my presence.

DAVID LLOYD

Cows Near Berllanderi, Wales

Digestion takes forever.
So does staring at hills,
minute by minute shadings.

If cool – they lie down.
If hot – they stand.
Chewing is a lifetime pursuit.
Magpies, their day-long companions.

Sex, a violent spasm, it's true,
but occasional, then the burden slides off.

Their massive, warm, hairy bodies.
Their slow, curious snouts.
Their teats filling with milk through the night.

Roused by the farmer's prod,
their calves close by,
they don't complain much, one field to the next,
tails flicking flies as best they can,
crowding to the never long enough trough.

When they turn their huge heads towards you,
they see you. They blink.
And then you're gone.

B.A. VAN SISE

Intensive Care Unit

In a perfect world, like this is,
the fan in my hospital room teetering,
tottering, tilting off the ceiling with a
click, click, click, click sounds

like a cricket, chirping in
the night along the dark road, sounds like
Clinton Corners. My aunt's farm, her field,
her horses, Sounds like ten years old-

my socks up against the glass, my
father driving the old red Mercury
over a road that groans. Sounds
like the rustling of animals in the

woods, fearful, watching to see
what happens, Sounds like skittish
scattering paws as the car
pauses at a corner, because it

sounds like they're certain
he's aiming, arming, but
he's just lost, in the dark,
even though he's been

here before. But then he
finds the road that winds
down to the old red house,
down its gray gravel drive,

and the lights turn on as
my aunt hears us arrive,
and the deer and the wolves
and the bats stay alive for

one more night. But here
the fan just whines and whines.
Sounds like the man in the next bed
is dying. Sounds like he doesn't mind.

B.A. VAN SISE

Reggie

My father carried the dog—
already, then, full of tumors,
half his weight disappeared
into breath— up in his arms like
he'd lumped sticks into a burlap
bag, over the threshold into
the veterinarian's office. The young
woman at the counter said Reggie was
a weird name for a dog, sounded
more like it should be on a
Black boy. Asked my father for the
dog's birthdate, which he didn't know.
Something about her files. Something
about she couldn't tell him because
of patient privacy and the dog,
who Dad adopted to be with him after he
moved back home in '71, didn't remember.
No, couldn't say. No, didn't remember. And
she told him he'd have to find out and
come back,
so Dad leaned down to the chair, poured
the dog into his arms, and carried him
out of there dying, draped over his elbows,
just like that boy in Viet Nam.

DANIEL LASSELL

Chair

Witnessed space,
a form before this made form.
Maybe, a lesson.
That things can change and still
assist, find purpose. I sit in it.

AMANDA HODES

Dark Tourism

"These sites may seem completely unmediated, but in fact, they are—just not there."

– Historian Gary Reger

we drop into the highway's seam
press our cheeks against asphalt
detect   an aftertaste of heat

how close can skin get to fire
before nerves crackle   or the body
instincts itself away?

cigarettes in the bull thistle
say *close*   spray-painted
hands gripped to pavement

closer   a couple
prunes Heineken bottles
from cemetery weeds   traces

gas pipes   to a blueprint of loss
a Jeep eyes the townhome's
        buttressed ribs

like a carcass   already
bone-pink clean
        he lowers his visor turns

from thick rewilding that leaves
nothing   only sidewalks to trees
stop signs   soft curtains of rain

now the lone memorial is a green
stenciled bench   so popular online
chained so it can't break free

* * *

I'd read the term   *dark tourism*
was coined the year I was born
            tourists had flooded Chernobyl

to buy glow-in-the-dark shirts
and Pringles cans   before donning masks
but in Centralia

buildings were bulldozed as a household left
to avoid squatters   perhaps
or pilgrimage

outside Mary's   our teenage heads buoy
beneath the window   spying
on the service

        Kate kneels in silt
between resin crosses and gravestones
to photograph names she's never met

I'm reminded of daguerreotypes
in thrift stores   their lace cuffs
and thin-plaited hair

how I divined their faces   like tea leaves
grainy smelling of oolong
and wood pulp   I wanted to see

just a glimpse of the congregation
but they funneled into cars
disappeared down the roads like a web

* * *

Graffiti Highway   reeks of Reddit
        some postmodern Bosch
or Dante's Inferno

a pubescent boy poses
with his Hurley cap   reaching
from the cracks

         easy to aestheticize
trespass   like the path of penises
redrawn on the blacktop daily

parents stroll their puffer-coat children
         through the throb of ATVs
Kate flashes pictures

         confession   song lyric   initials
everyone leaving their mark or
taking it with them

Centralia   named a *hidden gem*
of Pennsylvania
as if there's anything left to mine

when the sun sets like any east coast autumn
we lie   and say it's especially red
drive home

         playing B104 pop charts
to thumb through the photographs we've
taken

HILDE WEISERT

Portrait

The turkeys that I photographed last night—
fanned out on my south lawn, perusing
oddments in the scruffy end-of-summer grass,
each intent on its own hunt, unflappable
until my human shadow sounded an alarm,
shuddered them fluttering, high-stepping
into one hurry-up line racing headlong toward
the trees, and through the forest door—

—Flock this morning into my mind, mind waking
to the "plocka- plocka" of a gun, dull shots
out of sight. September, and turkeys mere creatures
with no alien intelligence to thrill to—not crows,
octopi, or pigs, not dolphins, or even bees—
just turkeys; nor beautiful like the peacock
or great blue heron that raise human hopes
of nature's consolations. Ungrievable

gawky dinner-birds, once turkeys on my lawn,
an ordinary family captured in my lens.

HILDE WEISERT

The Reach

"We are finding that the digits and the fin rays have some sort of equivalence at the level of the cells that make them. Honestly, you could have knocked me over with a feather."

– Neil Shubin, evolutionary biologist, University of Chicago

Glowing, their bones lie side by side.
The x-ray illuminates a human hand
beside its almost twin—a zebrafish fin,

and irradiation reveals a deep, shared story:
One embryonic aspiration reaching
the destined end of each appendage,

as buds bloomed into bone (dermal there,
endochondral, here)—fin rays to swim
unknowable depths,

or five fingers to reach
for words to grasp
the radiant kinship of their origin.

NATHALIE ANDERSON

Moonlight

after Ralph Albert Blakelock's paintings, circa 1883–1889
"Often I am permitted to return to a meadow."

—Robert Duncan

How many times has the full moon surprised you,
rising unexpected from a stand of trees, a roofline,
pulling the clouds across its face, trailing that veil
until the sky glows entire, a snowbank, a moonstone?

He was never surprised. Knew to the instant,
to the precise needle of pine, just where and when
to look for moonrise. Wherever he was,
whether road, or town, or wilderness.
Often I am permitted, he'd say, *to return.*

A night like this gets under the skin of the mind.
This pooling light – it's what we see
as sleep comes on, if sleep came on that way,
if we could watch it coming. How many times

painting it, painting it, painting it? Thinking one sees
more than one sees, more than there is to see.
Tree with a bend in its back, each leaf lit soft from above.
A leaning in. A watching over. Siloam.

Why then the scraping, the scoring, the clawing out,
the rubbing down, the scumbling, the pumicing?

Over every placidity, he'd say, a scouring wind.
What we see is overlay, is scrim, is veil, is cloud.
He'd do anything, anything, to get behind it, get
to the bottom of it. Again. Again. How often permitted?

NATHALIE ANDERSON

Egrets

René Lalique, "Aigrettes" vase, 1926

1.

Have you been there in the half-light
when morning warms towards day, and mist
thins off the marshes? I think I must have been,
the thick air familiar as a warm hand
on an arm; and the tang of brine, the swirl
of shrimp in the brine underfoot, muck
sucking foot from sandal : a girl
with a seine net seining shrimp
for her breakfast – yes, I think I
must have been there. And off inland
nearer the tree-line, breeze whispering
a susurrus of reeds, meticulously
moveless, yet swirling and pearly
as a mist gone feathery : egret.

2.

Lalique's been there too. Can't you tell? Watch
the glass of this vase, its thicks and its thins,
the settling weight of the mist pooled pearly
at its base, the sway and the weave
of its stalks of reed, bellying out and
curling over, and the lacy interlace
of its flocking birds : egrets, six to a side –
though no egrets I've ever seen: their chainmail
scales, their bladed wings, their snaking necks, their
piercing beaks and eyes : such seraphim! And yet
the exuberance of their tails – *more akin*
(says Eric Knowles) *to a bird of paradise* –
or are those leaves?, the sprays inextricable or
indistinguishable against the blue-grey staining.

3.

Nearly a century since its making.
Is it strange that I know what it went for

lately at auction? Three times my take-home
at the time. Do you blame me that I thought
seriously about it, think seriously about it
still? *Have nothing in your houses*, said
William Morris, famously, *that you don't know
to be useful or believe to be beautiful.* I swear
by that creed, yet doubt it. I live among treasures
in a time of treasures. If I opened my home
to these egrets, would I now be holy, rising
with them? Would that vase remind me daily
of something beyond itself – a visible symbol? Or
would it too become dusty, accustomed, merely daily?

NATHALIE ANDERSON

Ornithology at the Y

1.
Two birds at the window overlooking
the track, two birds every day looking in.

Two birds every day, and one of them rapt,
gazing in at whatever it's gazing at.

Two birds, finches, a nesting pair, not
nesting yet, and one of them rapt, one un-rapt,

by which I mean baffled. The glass baffles, it
deflects, and she can't see around it, or under, or in,

can't see what the rapt one gazes at. Baffled,
she tries sitting still, tries side-to-side steps,

tries angling her neck, tries queries, a peck
at his shoulder, shoulder peck, wing peck, tail peck,

but it's a stand-still stand-off: he's heedless, pre-
occupied, elsewhere, rapt, gazing still at whatever he's

still gazing at.

2.
I can't see what he sees. What I see
is this: industrial curtain, wall-high,
walling track off from racquet court. Thick

curtain, rubberized, stiff, but still restless,
still rustling when struck, say, on its far side
by a loose volley. Darksome, darkling, the shade

some call *bottle*, some *forest* – deep forest,
Black Forest – but the curtain's umbrous surface comes
scored with fine striations that, twitched or trembled,

glint the eye. As when needles of pine
sheen a windy hillside – is it that candle-lit
darkness he's lost in, rapt in, the curtain stirring

as when, say, I limp past, a puff of smoke,
a drift of mist among against the conifers –
or so I imagine he might see me.

3.
Purple finch, house finch: whichever, the male
is reddish, the female dull. Weeks later, I
honestly can't remember which bird – rapt
or antsy – was the rosy one, which the dun.

So is it my own residual binary
which assumes it's the male bird gazing
into space, into air, into the primordial,
the unreachable, untouchable, ineffable

when in my own times – oh
what's behind that curtain? – I was the one
so obsessed, so enticed by *isn't*
that I had no time or space for *is*.

4.
Weeks later, three birds at the window,
one reddish, two brown. I have no idea
what kind of engagement I'm gazing at.
This dun one's surely a girl, her mouth

full of vedge, urgent for nest or nestling –
displaced, baffled, frantic – and at either shoulder

(neck peck, wing peck, tail peck) the other two
query and quarrel and seek to steer her. The rosy one

is surely a male finch, but the other – larger,
rounder – looks more like a sparrow, and heck

the dun one could be a sparrow too. So,
two finches and a sparrow? two sparrows

and a finch? A boundary dispute? A romance
between species? An innovation
among genders? A *menage a trois*?
I'll never know. They're there only a moment

before they're flown.

5.
And all of this nothing to the starling
that's found its way inside: lap after lap
I pass the window where it's hunched
unmoving, inconsolable, gazing out rapt
at the unreachable real.

THOMAS MCGOWAN

A Tribute to R.T. Smith

R.T. Smith was a member of a stable of young writers at Appalachian who thrived under the whimsical mentorship of John Foster West in the 1970s. He went on to a distinguished career as an award-winning poet and fiction writer, editor of important literary reviews, teacher and writer-in-residence and encourager of writers. But he always maintained gracious loyalty to his writer friends and old teachers at Appalachian.

PHILLIP BELCHER

No Better Teacher

I am late submitting this to *Cold Mountain Review* and writing it has been harder than I expected. It feels like a formal "goodbye," and I do not want to say that. I miss Rod every day. I enjoyed him and learning from him, and there was always more to learn. There still is. His books are waiting for me to reread, and I will. It seems always to be the case that poets and their poems fade more quickly than they should. That is certainly the case with Rod. It was the case well before he died, and he knew it. Rod was a talented fiction writer, essayist, and poet, but I will always think of him as a poet first.

I met Rod in 2007; maybe it was 2008. I audited a residency workshop he was teaching at Converse University (née College). In our scheduled out-of-class meeting, Rod put me at ease and made me feel like I could be a poet. He made me feel like I had something to say and the talent to say it. He took me seriously and helped me understand that writing is more about effort than innate ability. He suggested that I attend the Sewanee writers' conference, where I met and studied all too briefly with Claudia Emerson and Mark Jarman, and suggested I think about an MFA. Two years later, in 2009, Rod became my primary mentor in Converse's inaugural creative writing MFA program, along with Sarah Kennedy, the Shakespeare scholar, poet and novelist who was also Rod's wife; Denise Duhamel; and Denise's then husband, the poet Nick Carbó. I loved working under their tutelage, and I have remained connected with Sarah and Rod until today.

Here is a sentence by Rod from his note on a poem in the 2002 Pudding House Greatest Hits series issue devoted to Rod's poems from 1975-2001: "Auden wrote that poetry makes nothing happen, but I'm convinced that language does cause things to happen, and so can poems, just as writing can confer further shape on experience, and the scrupulous ordering can give birth to power." Rod believed in language; he believed in precision; and he believed in the wild. He once told me that there was something in me that needed to let go—that some internal constriction kept my poems from flowering, from opening into what they could be. I'm still working on it, but Rod would not yet be satisfied.

Rod was a passionate man. If you knew him, you knew at least some of his likes and dislikes. He had a subtle mind. He loved the South but was not limited by it and understood the literary and professional pitfalls of being labeled "regional." He loved wild places and animals; one of the last books he recommended to me was Barry Lopez's *Of Wolves and Men*. He loved stories and told them better than anyone I've ever known. He was not afraid of voicing his dislikes, either. He mourned the homogeneity of the South, and he despised the vulgarity of the political currents that dominated his last years. He despaired of the lack of critical thinking that suffuses modern American culture.

Selfishly, I am going to miss all that I could have learned from Rod had he remained healthy until a much older age. He did not flaunt his knowledge of literature and its creators and continually surprised me. Not until one of our last conversations did I learn that he had known and interviewed another poet hero of mine, Hayden Carruth. I don't believe I knew until I read Rod's prose description of his poem "Yonosa House" while preparing this remembrance that he had Native American lineage. And I only got a glimpse of his understanding of, and love for, the Irish poets, especially Heaney.

I could go on for pages, but Rod would not stand for the sentimentality that would inevitably creep in. I'll close then by noting only that Rod was a brilliant and deeply humane man, a kind and gentle teacher who for nearly twenty years allowed me to call him my friend.

JIM STRAMM

A Tribute to R.T. Smith

When R.T. left ASU to go to Auburn (around Fall, 1976), he asked his friend Jack Dillard to take over as editor of *Cold Mountain Review* 5. Jack did most of the work on the edition, culling through submissions and making selections, but before the volume was published, he had to leave Boone in August 1977, as his wife had taken a job in Charlotte. Jack asked me if I would take the submissions of number 5 and oversee its publishing.

At the time I was a rising senior in the undergraduate English department and had no prior publishing experience. I had very little knowledge of *CMR* except what Jack had told me about R.T. I told him I was honored to help, but admitted I was clueless as to how to proceed. Jack suggested I talk with Professor Tom McGowan in the English department as Tom had helped guide the publishing of previous volumes. Tom was extremely helpful and led me to Tom Coffey in the University print shop. I handed over the submissions to Tom and the print shop and a few weeks later Number 5 was printed.

Throughout this process I had collaborated with good friend and fellow undergraduate English major, Dave Cook. Dave and I had started the ASU English Club in the Spring of 1977—an informal "club" comprised of a dozen or so fellow English majors. We would meet periodically to read each other's writings and drink beer. After number 5 was printed and distributed, a question arose as to who would edit and take responsibility for the next volume, Number 6. No one in the English graduate program was inclined, so Dave and I broached the subject with members of the English Club asking if they would be willing to help. Everyone was enthusiastically on board with the idea.

Before the club went any further, however, Dave thought that we should connect with R.T. to get his blessing that a team of undergrads would take over his pride and joy journal. Thus, during one of our club meetings we called R.T. He was initially disappointed that no graduate students were involved in *CMR* and was not sure that a bunch of undergrads had the requisite seriousness to organize and publish the journal. We assured him that we would put in the required effort and would work closely alongside Tom McGowan and other English faculty to complete the project. He reluctantly gave his blessing.

Editing and managing Number 6 turned out to be a wonderful experience for all of us involved. We published a handsome volume that we were all proud of in May 1978. Several weeks after publication we received a positive review from R.T., essentially saying he was happy that we didn't botch the job and tarnish the legacy of *CMR*. He appreciated us taking up the mantle and carrying on the tradition. We were gratified to get his positive feedback, knowing it meant a lot to him that *CMR* didn't stop.

CMR continued to be a product of both ASU English graduate and undergraduate students for many years thereafter. The spirit of R.T. lived on in each edition.

ALLEN SPEAR

So Long, It's Been Good to Know You

I remember Rod and I listening to Robert Penn Warren and Cratis Williams swapping stories. It was at the home of Dr. Richter Moore, Chair of the Political Science Department at Appalachian State University. Moore invited students and faculty to his home for a party. Warren and Williams, big-brained intellectuals, proceeded to delight, instruct, and entertain us. I asked Warren if he knew Richard Weaver from Weaverville, NC and what he thought of him. Weaver taught at the University of Chicago and was an icon of conservative scholars. Warren replied, "Yes I know him, but I'm afraid he's a bit of a cold fish." That's all he said to me. But I had the impression there was more to it than that. Did he think that Weaver's book, *Ideas Have Consequences*, was as cold and abstract as Weaver himself.

I also remember what Cratis said, although I heard his words years later. "The Appalachian Region," he said, "is becoming a nest of songbirds." Songbirds are not cold and abstract, they only sing. R.T. Smith was surrounded by songbirds. Poet John Thomas York worked with Rod on the first issue of the *Cold Mountain Review* in 1973. Hilda Downer, a talented young poet, had just started publishing her work. Charles Frazier, future winner of the National Book Award for his novel *Cold Mountain*, was Rod's best friend. Chuck, Rod, and Donald Secreast – Don was another fine writer—were joined at the hip it seems. When I saw one, I saw all three. Like the time they were filing in the front door of Hubie Williams' party in Boone. "There they are," I thought, " Rod, Don and Chuck; maybe three is a mystical number." These three, plus many others in the Boone area at the time, became award winning writers, scholars, and activists.

Rod was at the center of this circle of writers. He inspired me to write poetry but to no avail; I was a failed poet. But I did work on the *Cold Mountain Review* with David Cook and Debbie England. Rod was not impressed with our work. He said we ruined his magazine.

In spite of all that, Rod and I remained close friends. He encouraged me to start a little magazine at Lees-McRae College. I called it *Hemlocks and Balsams*. (One of my friends called it *Ham Hocks and Bullshit*.) Rod and I continued meeting in the 1980s. He was a frequent visitor to Lees-McRae. He came to the college to share his work with students in the honors program and continued to do so until the early 1990s.

Who knows how time, place, books, and especially people, create an alchemy of creativity. Rod was a catalyst for this creative energy. Cratis read the tea leaves right. "A nest of songbirds" resides in these mountains of ours and is ubiquitous in the Southern Appalachian region. Appalachian State University in the 1970s was indeed– in the words of Robert Penn Warren– *A Place to Come To.*

CHARLES FRAZIER

R.T. Smith—A Few Episodes From a Half-Century Friendship

By way of preface, I've been credited over the years with being one of the group led by Rod and including Donald Secreast, who began *Cold Mountain Review* at ASU back in the nineteen-seventies; I was not. I never even submitted work—mainly because among that group I was the scholar, with no poetry or fiction to submit. I had, though, read Han Shan via Gary Snyder, and still have my original, faded and very used copy of *Rip Rap And Cold Mountain Poems*. So, while I intended my novel, *Cold Mountain*, to be colored by Snyder's translation, the mountain of my book is the one here in western North Carolina. You can hike to its 6030 foot summit on a through trail beginning a mile from what was once my grandfathers' hunting camp.

In 1973 Boone, there were two rooming dumps close to campus with academic sounding names: Ivy Hall and College Hall. Rent at the cheaper of the two, College, where I lived, was $135 per quarter—a quarter being defined as a three-month unit of the academic calendar. You reached College Hall up a narrow set of stairs on King Street next door to the movie theater. My monkish room had a metal single bed, a small closet, and a very dingy gas-station-style sink. A grimy toilet and shower were a dim walk down the hall.

Rod and Don lived a block away in Ivy, maybe a degree or two nicer and slightly more expensive than College. They were both teaching assistants, which meant that the university paid them rather than the other way around. And they got an office, a big room in the English building with maybe nine desks. We grad students without assistantships were close to invisible.

So, I wrote a good paper and presented it in a twentieth-century poetry class. I wrote it specifically to show off, to step up and earn an assistantship. Heads up! Here's what I can do. I wish I still had the paper, because in many ways it changed my future and led to some of the most important and defining friendships of my life, including my wife, Katherine. Professor Coulthard liked the paper and Don—also a student in the class—did too. I didn't know him at the time, but he climbed the dark steps to College Hall to compliment my work. The way I remember it, Don and Coulthard talked it up around the English department, concluding I was worthy of an assistantship.

Rod de facto ran the TA part of the department, and when he invited or summoned me to a meeting in his Ivy Hall room, it felt like a job interview. Soon after I entered his room, he said, What current poets do you read?

I'm sure I started with Snyder. Probably threw in James Wright and Galway Kinnell.

Rod said, "What about W.S. Merwin?"

I said, "Haven't read him."

He reached to his bedside table and shuffled a stack of thin paperbacks and frisbeed across the room a copy of *The Lice*. He said, "Tell me what you think about it."

Some might have felt a little threatened or insulted—Rod could have that effect—but I was intrigued. I wanted to know this guy. There was clearly something to be learned.

For an immediate confirmation of that now, all I have to do is glance at the bookshelf across from my writing desk, where, along with numerous other Merwin books, are two copies of *The Lice*.

Next quarter, I became a TA, cashing a whopping check every month from ASU, and sharing an office with Rod and Don. That office had a gravity that pulled people in. We were deadly serious about literature and writing, and that drew others who also felt the pull. My future wife Katherine would sometimes drift through after a dance class, her dark hair pulled back, and all the guys in the room paused to notice. And I remember Debbie England, now a dear friend, then a freshman with a great big smile (still present) and who later became one of the students who kept *Cold Mountain Review* going after Rod and Don moved on to academic and writing careers. (Don, by the way, arranged my first date with Katherine and performed all the functions at our wedding other than the ones North Carolina law required to be done by a real preacher.)

Typical of Rod's impulse to keep things lively, one day he came over to my desk and said, "I just ran into Trimpey, and he asked me what you were reading. I told him you were big into contemporary Mexican drama." Rod had among his repertoire of smiles a sort of wolfish grin, thin vertically, but extending back to the molars. Again, this is where some took offense. I wanted to play the game Rod had set before me. And also, like most of the grad students, I wanted to impress Professor Trimpey, who I knew would question me about contemporary Mexican drama the next time I saw him. I knew zero about Mexican drama, old or new. So I spent every spare moment for a few days dodging Trimpey and reading everything the ASU library had on the subject. When Trimpey asked me the inevitable questions, I made the most of my hard-won, fingernail-thin new knowledge. When I reported back to Rod, he was delighted, mostly I think, because I had taken up the gauntlet rather than just ratting him out to Trimpey. It was a part of Rod that I liked the most, the mixture of playfulness and challenge.

That countermove helped set the tone for our new friendship. By the time Katherine and I married a couple of years later, Rod's cryptic guest register sign-in as "R.T. Smith, skeptic" didn't give us a moment's pause.

Years later I had gone by myself down into the Copper Canyon in northern Mexico. I was scouting for another travel book like the one I'd written with Don on the northern Andes—Ecuador, Peru, Bolivia. Copper Canyon's magic proved a bit a darker than Peru's, so I reconsidered and climbed out to the canyon rim, hitched rides to the nearest little dirt road town, and took a series of buses north to El Paso, where I'd left my car. A bit at loose ends, I remembered Rod was spending the summer up in Taos having a writing retreat, but I had no idea how to find him. This, of course, all occurred in a world still free of cell phones.

So I drove a few hundred miles up to Taos to drop in on Rod, if I could find him. I pictured him way out in the mountains in a little cabin. I was just going to show up, have dinner and drinks, leave the next day so as not to disturb the retreat. When I drove into Taos, wondering where to start, at the very first red light, Rod walked across the street in front of me. I blew the horn, leaned out the window and yelled, "Get out of the road, idiot."

Rod had no idea I was anywhere within fifteen hundred miles, but it was immediately like he had an itinerary in mind for a several day visit. With a backpack full of gear, I camped in the living room of his little cottage—vigas and latillas and a tiny fireplace. One of the activities was to drive a long way out to Abiquiu to see the village and drive by Georgia O'Keeffe's house. Back then it was still a private residence—no guided tours, no visitor's center. Just circle it real slow and think, A creative genius once lived here. We also went on hikes, climbed up to cliff dweller ruins, went to several little pottery villages, and talked nonstop about books and writing and writers. It was that kind of friendship— no need to waste time reestablishing it after gaps of time. Just pick up where you left off. I still have an exquisite piece of black San Illdefonse Pueblo pottery I bought from some lady's living room during that visit. It's perfect, the size of a tennis ball, a beautiful remembrance of that day, and it has ever since been one of my writing desk talismans.

End of summer in 2001, Rod called with the somber news that he had cancer and was going through a stretch of five-day-a-week radiation treatments. So I went up to Lexington, and for a week I drove him down to the hospital in Roanoke for his treatments. The first day was 9/11. I'll never forget watching the horrific news on TV in a waiting room where sick people and their families had plenty to worry about already.

Every afternoon Rod came out of radiation with a clear sense of how many hours and fractions of hours he'd continue to have an appetite and the ability to hold down food, so he'd pack in as many calories as he could. An immediate milk shake at Sonic, and then we'd follow the Blue Ridge Parkway back to Lexington, stopping for a chili dog along the way. On those drives it was hard to anticipate whether he wanted to talk and if so, what he might want to talk about, but where Rod got most engaged was talking about writers, musicians, artists. Bob Dylan's *Love and Theft* was released that week. I bought it at a record store in Lexington one morning so we could listen and discuss in the car if he was interested. Which he was, even laughing at some of Dylan's sly humor.

Months later at one of the milestones in cancer treatment, Rod called and said he'd gotten an all clear, and that Barry Lopez was going to be around for a campus visit and reading in Lexington. He said, "Come up and we'll do the things we do." And he meant do those things without cancer hanging so heavy over every moment.

But here's the backstory to that trip to Lexington in 2002. It goes back to 1978, the year Barry Lopez's *Of Wolves And Men* was published. Katherine and I were working on doctorates at University of South Carolina, and Rod was teaching at Auburn. Once or twice a year I'd head to Alabama to spend a few days with Rod. That '78 trip, we had both read the Lopez book and were blown away by it, talked on and on about it and its author. One day we drove to a way-out-in-the-country barbecue joint, where the sides of the cinder-block building were muraled with a colorful flock of chickens above jagged letters reading, the only way to get a better piece of chicken is to be a rooster. Inside, incongruously—or so it seemed to us at the time—a woman sat on a stool at the register reading *Of Wolves And Men*. We couldn't resist asking, "How come you're reading that book?" And she said, "Because my nephew wrote it."

Well, we wondered about that puzzling encounter for more than two decades. Barry Lopez had seemed so west coast, so vast, redwoods not red clay, a writer hero on the elevated plain of Gary Snyder. A world apart from Opelika, Alabama. In the decades between Opelika and sitting in Rod and Sarah's living room with Barry, I had become acquainted with him, but I'd never brought up the barbecue story. If Rod and I couldn't tell it together, I'd rather not tell it at all.

So there we were, and together we told Barry the story, and he said, "Oh that was my aunt." So, more anticlimactic than we had imagined, no story at all, really, but somehow perfect for that little thread of shared narrative to play out as it did, maybe a lesson in how most writers turn out to be less exotic than you imagine them to be.

By the way, one thing we almost never did was talk about the oddity of my having written a novel topping bestseller lists for long stretches of time and winning the National Book Award. What was there to say? Ask us in 1973 and we'd have declared all that stuff secondary to everything we thought important about writing, and it remained so.

Rod was one of the greatest shaping forces of my life, and I send out to him—into the afterworld or the ether or wherever there is to send out to—waves of gratitude and love. Thanks for fifty years of words, poems, books, laughs, friendship. Who could ask for more, other than for more time?

JIM MINICK

Onions

The onions arrive in early April, slips the size of pencils—white rootlets at the tip instead of graphite, green leaves round and alive instead of yellow hexagons of wood.

Each already holds a tear.

I work the bed by hand, three-pronged cultivator to loosen the soil, rake to pull and shape, hoe to furrow, finger to poke and plant. It is a long sheet of dark paper. I am writing my name. The soil is soft and still cool from winter, the sky gray and headstrong with wind. I wear flannel, wool, and rain jacket, and halfway through, the patter comes. Three days of heavy rain is predicted, so if I don't get the onions in now, the soil will be too wet for days after and these plants will wither. There are over 400 green pencils. They came from Texas, and already, they have wilted leaves from the 1400-mile trip. I keep working through the drizzle. Mud cakes my fingers.

The bundles are rubberbanded together—yellow for keepers, purple for sweet. I poke the purple close for thinning and green-onion eating in a month or two. The keepers get more space. As spring becomes summer, the tears will grow, the layers thicken. The tablet of dirt will expand to make room for each pencil writing itself into a knuckle, a marble, a thick-skinned globe. In the basement, seven onions sit in their almost empty crate, keepers from last season. At dusk, I will pull two from their nested place and start peeling, tan husk of skin three layers thick opening to ring upon ring, white packed translucence, flavor and health too strong to eat raw. Scent on fingertips too strong for soap. A full moon in my palm. My knife a letter-opener, I slice open each one. I can never read what is inside. I weep every time.

TREY HALL

Silo Tree on Catawba Road

As soon as I hear my old pickup putter a low rumble, I forget about the ENT visit I'm running from. I park out front of my childhood home and ditch my pollen-stained Subaru. Dad is waiting just outside the barn, and we head straight for the 1986 Jeep Comanche we rebuilt when I was a kid, pearlescent paint, barbed wire pinstripe, true dual exhaust. The engine roars when I drop the clutch shifting out of reverse into first. We cruise up Hollymeade, down Coventry, then right onto my favorite backroad.

Catawba winds through a crevice between ridges. Pastures and abandoned mills sit between stained glass churches and old farmhouses. We listen to "Willie and the Boys," the album Willie Nelson released with his two sons, Lukas and Micah, singing the songs of Hank Williams and Hank Snow, the songs Dad sang to me as a child. Dad belts out, sliding between melody and harmony, and I mouth the words, my throat still throbbing from the ENT.

Willie's voice is worn as over-dried leather. Weathered and ragged, yet beautiful. He sings with his sons in blood harmonies. Kinfolk share a melody like no other. Dad and I sink deeper into the plush tan bench seat. The broken seat belt clips thrash against the door panels as we hug turns on a road with less than two lanes. A creek paves the outer lip of the roadside, the bank splotched with shades of green.

My throat is raw from getting scoped at the doc, so I sit silent, one hand on the wheel, the other resting on the gear shift. Dad turns down the music and says "Well boy, you just never know," answering a question I hadn't asked aloud. His drawl thick as the honeysuckle lining Catawba Road. Tires hum atop asphalt, I swerve around roadkill, the carcass of a possum splattered on pavement. He tacks on, "Hell, I lost my voice for six … months … silent," drawing out his words, emphasizing each one.

Dad isn't trying to say it could be worse. He's saying he gets it. Memories of vocal polyps flash in Dad's sunlit eyes. A surgeon's blade cutting too deep. Months of silence. A notepad he used to order food or talk to a barber or argue with a speech therapist, ink becoming a new voice.

With his arm resting out the window, Dad says, "You know, it takes time. And shit man, time only knows." Burn scars from cancer glint his skin. I wish I'd brought sunscreen for the both of us. Dad's red hair has faded to a solid silver, now long enough to touch the soft of his back. My hair is still red, not yet polished by time's metallic hues. Our skin is pale and freckle-licked, both arms glowing red from the bite of sunlight.

I keep on, grimace and nod, grimace and nod, clutch and gas, clutch and gas. The air passing through the truck cab is too loud for me to talk over. I weave between ridges and memories. Dad says, "But I'm tellin ya, once you're all fixed up, we better get to recordin somethin. Cause I'ma die and my voice'll go with me." Dad's candor shakes me. He is usually the stoic type, only speaking of death as a joke. I glance away from the road to look at him. He stares out the window framed by mountains, the scruff of his beard wind-kissed. Willie & the Boys keep singing quietly.

If we don't record, Dad's song will be a tombstone, a faded memory. All his 70 years, Dad's voice has never been recorded proper, save a shoddy phone video or VHS. I try to shake off dark thoughts. The road straightens up, overlooks a rolling valley. Memories pour in his voice blaring from the stacked speakers at Galax. A canary yellow tent casts a glow on everything underneath. Riding on Dad's shoulders as he walked the festival grounds in braided leather Jesus sandals, holding my knees with palms the size of my entire thigh. Mom wearing denim overall shorts, holding my small, not yet calloused fingers. Flatfooting on sheets of plywood. Mom's laughter mixing with dust. The clapper and clank of shoes drumming to the band. Dad's voice brimming over Felts Park. A pin-point turn takes my attention and I swerve back into my body.

We park the truck on a gravel shoulder that doubles as the parking lot for Mountain View Baptist. Dad and I aren't the church going type, but the view up here is a real slice. The closed doors echo across the pasture facing the church. Dad walks just ahead of me. We climb toward a shelter with picnic tables, a barbeque grill, bird nests tucked in every corner. I've only ever heard Dad speak of god in song, the same way these birds surrounding us must. My only spiritual connection is through the folk songs we sing. Or I guess, used to sing. Pain tends to question itself. Have I lost my god? Is the sound of heaven dead? Is it sleeping in a scar on my right vocal fold?

Sitting atop a moss and grime painted picnic table, Dad hums to himself, the car speakers still ringing in his ears long after I cut the engine. We unroll tin foil covered biscuits Mom made, steam and butter waft, filling the air. We chew slowly, comfortably silent, and the music shifts to bluejays fluttering around us. Their voices replace ours. Dad forgets his surgical silence. I settle into unknowing.

We lick our fingers clean, brush crumbs on our jeans, spark a joint, rest our elbows on the bowed 2x4s lining the tabletop. Dad is a storyteller. Between drags, he tells me about Willie Nelson and Johnny Paycheck in 1980, how they canceled a festival last minute in Franklin County because the sheriff threatened to arrest Willie on the spot if he turned up a bottle on stage. So Willie and Johnny never stepped foot off the tour bus, must have just thought, "Take this job and shove it / I ain't working here no more," Dad breaks into song this part of the story as if on stage. He goes on, tells me how protests broke out. Longhairs and speed freaks and outlaws. Old barns burnt to the ground. Dad and Uncle Bobby split a fifth of Wild Turkey and watched them burn with a smile. The Airstream reflecting charred lumber and flame. Fire—the only song in Franklin County that day. They left as ashes smoldered, Dad pulling the Airstream down to his first Galax. He's gone to the fiddler's convention almost every year since.

We snuff out the roach and leave the peak. I drift the mountain in neutral, the truck's weight pushing us down the road. Without radio or birdsong, Dad breaks in, "Now I'll admit it, I done my share of screamin and hollerin. Prolly what gave me them blame polyps," his voice rumbles, words warbling between the tenor and bass of his range.

Clearing my throat, I say, "They said I got heavy scarring, muscle and nerve damage," I take a long draw of air, gulp water to coat my throat. "They threw round some other medical terms I can't remember, but it ain't good. Oh, and they said I prolly inherited a bad apple or two from you," I say with forced laughter and the accent I bury until I'm talking to my kin. The accent that blossoms when I sing. But the friction of laughter burns, stealing my smile.

We pass the graveyard of a cabin burnt down. The jagged teeth of a foundation. Scars to remember what once stood. The chimney standing alone now. I watch Dad struggle to respond, mulling over what I need to hear in this moment and knowing there isn't much to say. The gap in conversation weighs on him, I can tell he wants to tell me a story, something about survival, or maybe tell me about the family that died in that cabin, tell the story he's told me since I was a kid just about every time we pass the ruins.

I turn the radio dial and music pours out of the speakers. We listen to lineage, sound passed down from parent to child. Addiction and recklessness passed through nature and nurture. Without much thought, Dad mumbles, almost to himself, "Gawt-blame Willie's voice done lost its boom. Guess time'll wear ya down," his silver hair keeps on shining. Time repairs our wounds only to untether them. The song, the sound, the vibration, all temporary.

Dad stares at a dilapidated silo on the horizon. From the top of the silo, a small tree grows out a hole in the roof. Its arms reach toward the blue. Bark burning in sunlight, roots burrowed into corroding brick and mortar. I imagine a bluejay nest settled on one of the branches. Its song reverberates through the silo.

DARIA-ANN MARTINEAU

Why I Write Poetry

A prehistoric urge
draws the leatherback up from such depth
it would crack the shell of another turtle.
Instead, time has covered her spine
with ridged skin. Tough but feeling.
Each year she pulls her nine hundred pounds,
her centuries of weight
to a shore far from where she began.
All to empty her belly into fine-grain earth,
bury her descendants
under the moon. Each perfect pale sphere
a life with a chance to emerge,
to hatch open and live
through the swooping of mongoose
and shorebird. Always,
a few make it back to the water.
They, too, become mothers—
a chance to return
& return.

DARIA-ANN MARTINEAU

Twenty-One

Return and flash again
flag I crushed beneath my heel. Perennial bulbs
in April bloomed a booming red
I loved you then, hopelessly,
to live amidst your fast changing earth and sky,
rainy and dry. How strange
where I came from, there were two seasons.
Starving in the lushness of the tropics
after weeks away, wanting you
I let you have me that January
fell soft at your bedroom window,
the leaves crumbled, then heaven
sticky as maple, as an amber trap
teacup nestled in your palm. You poured in
braced me for winter. I turned
your skin, brown like damp earth,
scented with whiskey, oak-barrel warmth
I entered this new year, heady
lilting winds kissed trees, bid them undress.

DARIA-ANN MARTINEAU

Rereading Beloved in the NICU

How brutally tender
like a mother's hand.
Even when my daughter is cut
from me, I am her home. Skin
on translucent skin,
we sit crib-side
under post partum's fluorescence,
eclampsia's wake. I wade
deep into escape and confrontation,
entangled like a chokecherry root.
EKG's cooing, pulse
oximeter's sudden wails.
I am her constant. I come back,
older, to this text. A different me,
mother now. I know the terror
of having someone to kill for.
This knowing absorbs me,
gnaws at my marrow.
Inside me, this child's need
had grown thick
'til my vessels filled almost to bursting.
I turn pages and my milk pulls down. Tears
drain my body. I push against the rush
of love, lamentation,
the entire Ohio River.
Everything stays with you. I know
I have crossed and can never
turn back to what was.

RON SMITH

He Said It Literally Saved His Life

True story, my friend said, holding up his right hand
  as if his left were on a King James.
  When the docs, nurses, orderlies
    found out I was un poeta—
  (un poeta maschio, his wife said, for some reason),
    —one by one they crept to my bedside,
male and female, with shining eyes, shy smiles, soft voices,
  said, I read some of your poesia online,
  said, molto bene, sometimes backing away as if
    from the pope or Mussolini.
    He said they came with tiny Italian-English
  dictionaries, checked his chart, his I.V.
      every few minutes.
Molto molto bene, said his wry wife.

      Back in the States,
   driving back at midnight
     from another sparse, polite audience,
on 95 just south of D.C., a truck drifted his way,
  he jerked the wheel, went perfectly sideways
on screaming dry pavement, then sideways other way,
    whipping too far into the skid, sideways
again and again, wondering now in that slo-mo calm
  why he hadn't yet flipped, thinking this time, *this*—
but finally nosing off into the weedy median, foreseeing
  a concrete culvert or something worse.

  The cop who saw it all said, You one lucky sucker,
   I swear I thought you'd flip, but I see why
     you didn't, pointing at the back
bench's mound of books, front and back floorboards
    heaped, three layers in the passenger seat.
My friend said, It's all poetry, I'm a poet, trunk's full, too.
Yep, you got blank verse ballast, cop said.
    You know some poetry, poet said.
Naw, cop said, just Robert Frost and what's her name—
   Dickens. Cop smiled: Who woulda
    thought poetry could save anybody's life?

He circled the Toyota with his flashlight
        one more time, said, I think you driveable.
That's when the poet told the story of nearly dying in Orvieto,
        cop leaning forward, watching his lips.
                You have any trouble getting home,
    he said, give me a ring, handing over a slip of paper
            with his neatly penned cell. Poet said, If I had
a clean copy of one of my *own* books, I'd sign it to you right now,
        Officer smiled, took back the paper,
                    wrote his address, said, Hell, you might be
        better'n life insurance.
    Sì, molto meglio, the poet's wife said,
                like a judge passing sentence.

RON SMITH

Know Ledge

after Louise Bogan

Now that you know
You can stand
Here without vertigo,
Without even a strand

Of hope belaying you
To the solid land,
What's delaying you
But cowardice and—

RON SMITH

Grace: Black Ice

None yet, though
the hot water pipes
have frozen three times

in a fortnight, our fort
in the night, strange to me

as the phrase black ice.
None. So. Far. No spin-
outs, no winterscape fro-

licking in the wind-
shield, no sliding side-

ways off the road. Insult-
ing, O yes, slap of the wind
from the door to the car,

from the car to the gym,
but no upsy-daisy feet flying

toward the sky, laughter
from the young, none
ever from older. No-

thing like the time I took one
step through the front door

toward the yellow plastic tube
on the frosted grass, saw tree
limbs, skulled loud thud that

was the back of my head hitting
bricks. Lay there a long two,

three, four seconds, assuming
if not the end, beginning
of the end, such a blow, smack

on the occipital, but found I
could stand, could small step into

our warm house, smelling somehow
freshly mowed lawns, only a smear
of cordial blood on my fingertips.

DAVID MARTIN

Legislation and a Rain Barrel

How global warming changed
the way we love, economized interactions,
brief attempts at being temporarily legible
to strangers, by post, comment or reply
the compounding of losses, confounding
bosses of industry, home alone,
relishing solitude, learning to bake bread,
discovering einkorn, making sauerkraut,
lamenting my decision to not raise chickens
this year, considering the wild turkeys
and mule deer, looking up wild game recipes
rehydrating the mushrooms I harvested
and praying for enough winter snowpack
or spring rain for there to be more this year,
and no, not praying for, not like that—
if we've learned anything the last few years
you cannot petition the lord through prayer,
but instead through policy, legislation
and a rain barrel, making a new tradition
of swapping seeds with friends and family
you see, you've got to come with respect
there's solace enough in the wilderness
to untrouble your head
just don't take your sorrows
to the dry creek bed

ANNA LAURA REEVE

Carolina Allspice

I'm freckling up. Wrinkling like a golden raisin.
Your hands still look young.
Mine look beautiful to me.

Tiny ants climb my laptop screen as the sun pulls hard
against late summer, trying to go down.

The brain, preoccupied with dark concerns.
Carried in a bucket with holes.

When it huddles over itself—shuddering,
leaking some too-viscous fluid—oh, to be free.

Symbols of nature, like the cardinal carrying a cicada
into the thicket, or the phoebe on the T-post
looking over the meadow,
fall away between us.

I'm afraid to say something too true,
afraid of the smallest lie.

The seed contains the truth; an alkaloid,
smelling of allspice and bay.

ANNA LAURA REEVE

Neotibicen Tibicen Tibicen

Morning cicadas scrape tinny eight-second phrases from the boxelders.
Four bars' crescendo, bow rasping hard into the string, horsehair

splintering, a gathering of light—or pain—then a diminuendo,
which the scissor-grinder cicadas' punctuating drone laps

like a tide going out, like the Gabrieli and Taverner motets I loved
as a teenager. Orlando Gibbons, who split one choir into many

balconies, his *Miserere mei*s and *humilitatem*s cascading and insistent.
At midday, dog-day cicadas awaken, buzzing a single brassy note.

Days cool, releasing damp breath, little by little. Like Gibbons,
hunched over a desk as plague years screeched and whistled outside

his windows, writing "Hosanna to the Son of David" by lamplight,
we make our own relief by calling out. *Listen, if you were here.*

Listen, whoever you are. A resolved chord building from balcony
left, answering balcony right, engulfing each other like waves.

ANNA LAURA REEVE

Self Portrait as Strength

I balance on a narrow bench while the sifu shouts
instructions for the lion dance over the class,

sharp claps falling into the roar of box fans like hail
into sand. I'm thinking about divorce, children

of two families, and whether to make my daughter
one of them. The kids make timed steps, kicks,

turns. They shout syllables, tiny elbows tucked,
while above them, sabers, knives, sickles, cherry

poles and a black tined pitchfork hangs on the wall.
Weapons studded around her, an enormous praying mantis

gazes from a painted banner, unlidded eyes staring,
and the Foshan lion, whose skin leaps and dances

over the legs of two teenagers, wiggles its tail.
Opens and closes and opens its mouth. And the rails

and banisters red, concrete floor redwashed a bright
crimson, matte and thick as blood halfway dried, rich

as blood that will not appear but ticks, safe as a clock
beneath everyone's soft skin.

DON JOHNSON

Singer

When I tell people my first car
was a Singer, they laugh,
sometimes, if they're sitting down,
bicycling their legs as if
they were pumping a treadle.
I did start it on occasion
with the crank stored
under the bonnet. And
the space between the doors
and convertible top created
so much space I plugged
the hole with an umbrella,
when the *mauka* showers swept
Manoa Valley. Sometimes I held
It in my teeth when shifting gears
and steering, which worked
when trade winds didn't blow.
In Honolulu, trade winds
always blow. I frequently
arrived wet, wetter when
I had to pull to the shoulder,
raise the hood, remove
the points from the distributor,
and sand their burned surfaces
with emery cloth. The aluminum
body was tacked to an oak frame'
bolted to the chassis, a plus
in the tropics, since it didn't rust.
But I had to treat the oak
for termites. I sold it
for a hundred dollars when I left
the islands in 1964. I'd give
ten times that to have her back.

DON JOHNSON

Shovel

Noun, verb, command,
each one applies
on this day so cold
water pipes freeze
below the frost line.
My shovel clangs
on topsoil like a dishpan
whacked with a wooden
spoon at a shivaree,
but even partly frozen
earth yields to this
oldest of tools, my most
antique implement,
the wooden-handled one,
not the newer spade
with the yellow plastic
shaft that sunlight fades.

This one's hickory handle
gleams from hard use,
palm sweat and body oil
rubbing the raised grain
to a fine patina. Lacking
the hayfork's pastoral glow,
the hoe's artistic glamour,
the shovel moves more
than earth. The deeper
the dig, the brighter shine
on its ordinary blade.

CATHERINE CHILDRESS

Standing on Lafayette Street

outside the hotel you chose because Lorca
is muraled on its facade, you smoke
a stale cigarette and wonder if locals
pronounce its name like Faulkner's county,
then think not, though both claim the same man—

about Ashbury and O'Hara whose poems
you've never understood except maybe
to say they are poems of place. This place
where the street is called *LA-fee-yette,*
where, on the N train, an old man peels an orange,

separates each carpel, takes one for himself,
passes the next to his wife. Again. Again,
until what's left is the gyre of rind
between them and their silence—
the eye of this underground hurricane,

where one dollar buys the city's best slice
and any donation is enough for a prayer
at St. Michael's altar— *mercy,*
no more cancer, safe flight—and spare change
tossed in a cup or open case is everything,

where you stand on this corner and watch
women choose from fruit heaped
on plywood—dragon, passion, sweet
pomelo—and long for the Delta-
drawl of your grandmother's la-FAY-ette
and canned fruit cocktail served syrupy
over cottage cheese in *Tobacco Leaf* china.

DORIANNE LAUX

Country

I can see my country from the window of my house,
the blooming promise of it, the watery undertow.
Everyone everywhere is in the middle, where all
the crooked roads meet. Our country has us
in its jaw, more in than out of its open mouth.
We are its lovely omens, its scruffy offspring.
Some of us stand in the shower, trying to scrub
ourselves clean, breaking the skin, bleeding a little,
repeating Let go, let go, but I don't know how.

CONTRIBUTORS

Nathalie Anderson

Nathalie Anderson's books of poetry include *Following Fred Astaire, Crawlers, Quiver, Stain, Rough, and the chapbook Held and Firmly Bound.* Her poems have appeared in *Atlanta Review, DoubleTake, Natural Bridge, The New Yorker, Nimrod, Plume,* and elsewhere. Anderson has authored libretti for five operas in collaboration with Philadelphia composer Thomas Whitman. She has recently retired from Swarthmore College, where she served as a Professor of English Literature, and directed the Program in Creative Writing.

Catherine Pritchard Childress

Catherine Pritchard Childress lives in the shadow of Roan Mountain in East Tennessee. She teaches writing, literature, and Appalachian Studies at Lees-McRae College. Her poems have appeared in *North American Review, The Cape Rock, Louisiana Literature, Connecticut Review, Appalachian Review, Still: The Journal,* and *Stoneboat* among other journals. Her work has also been anthologized in *The Southern Poetry Anthology,* Volumes VI and VII: Tennessee and North Carolina, and in *Women Speak,* Volumes VII and VIII. She is the author of *Other* (Finishing Line Press 2015) and *Outside the Frame* (Eastover Press 2023).

Trey Burnart Hall

Trey Burnart Hall is an MFA nonfiction/poetry student at Virginia Commonwealth University and the lead podcast editor of Blackbird. He is from Botetourt County but has been based in Richmond over a decade. Trey is a musician, producer, collaborator, educator, and community organizer, chairing the Parallel Listening Series at Gallery5 and hosting the EarthFolk Old-Time Jam. His production work and collaborations through his label, *Vocal Rest Records,* have been nominated for the Folk Alliance International Album of the Year, shortlisted for the Newlin Music Prize, archived in the Library of Congress as part of the 20th anniversary of the Richmond Folk Festival, and featured in NPR Live Sessions, Bandcamp Daily, and more. His archival photography project, *Wickline Speed Shop,* has been exhibited at the Alexander Heath Contemporary Art Gallery and Black Iris Social Club and will be featured in the 2025 Born-Free Motorcycle Show in Silverado, California. His academic work has been published in the *Journal of Inclusive Postsecondary Education* and presented at the Postsecondary Disability Training Institute and Southeastern Writing Center Association. He works as the VCU Writing Center Assistant Director and lives in the Southside of Richmond with his partner, Gray, and pup, Waylon.

Amanda Hodes

Amanda Hodes is a writer and new media artist. She currently teaches creative writing at Oberlin College & Conservatory. Winner of the 2024 Philip Levine Prize for Poetry, her debut collection *Into the Into of Earth Itself* is forthcoming from Black Lawrence Press in 2026. She has also been published in *Prairie Schooner, Pleiades, Black Warrior Review, AMBIT, Denver Quarterly, PANK,* and elsewhere.

Don Johnson

Don Johnson is retired from East Tennessee University after thirty years as professor, administrator, and Poet in Residence. His poems have appeared in journals such as *Poetry, Prairie Schooner,* and *The Iowa Review.* He has published four volumes of poetry, a novel, and numerous critical articles.

Daniel Lassell

Daniel Lassell is the author of *Frame Inside a Frame* (Texas Review Press, 2025) and *Spit* (Wheelbarrow Books, 2021), winner of the Wheelbarrow Books Poetry Prize. He is also the author of two chapbooks: *Ad Spot* (Ethel Zine & Micro Press, 2021) and *The Emptying Earth* (Madhouse Press, 2023), which was a finalist for the 2024 Medal Provocateur Award. He grew up in Kentucky, and now lives in Bloomington, Indiana. Visit his website at www.daniel-lassell.com.

Dorianne Laux

Dorianne Laux's sixth collection, *Only As the Day is Long: New and Selected Poems* was named a finalist for the 2020 Pulitzer Prize for Poetry. Her fifth collection, *The Book of Men,* was awarded The Paterson Prize. Her fourth book of poems, *Facts About the Moon,* won The Oregon Book Award and was short-listed for the Lenore Marshall Poetry Prize. Laux is also the author of *Awake; What We Carry,* a finalist for the National Book Critic's Circle Award; *Smoke;* as well as a fine small press edition, *The Book of Women.* She is the co-author of the celebrated text *The Poet's Companion: A Guide to the Pleasures of Writing Poetry.* Her latest collection of poetry is *Life On Earth* and was released in January of 2024. *Finger Exercises for Poets,* a book of concise craft essays and exercises for poets was released in July 2024.

David Lloyd

David Lloyd is the author of eleven books, including four poetry collections: *The Everyday Apocalyps*e, *The Gospel According to Frank, Warriors,* and *Shared Origins: a collaboration between three poets* (forthcoming from Seventh Quarry Press). His books of fiction include *Boys: Stories and a Novella, Over the Line* (a novel), and *The Moving of the Water* (stories). His poems, translations, and stories have appeared in numerous journals, including *Denver Quarterly, Massachusetts Review,* and *Virginia Quarterly Review.*

David Martin

David Anthony Martin is the author of four collections of poetry, most recently *The Ground Nest.* His poems and essays have appeared in *Bristlecone, One Sentence Poems, The Dewdrop, Cold Mountain Review* and others, as well as in several anthologies, most notably *The Literary Field Guide to the Rocky Mountain West*. He has published over 80 weekly articles in the Pueblo Chieftain's Nature's Classroom column. He is the founder & editor of Middle Creek Publishing & Audio.

Daria-Ann Martineau

Daria-Ann Martineau was born and raised in Trinidad and Tobago and holds an MFA in Poetry from New York University. She is an alumna of several writing conferences including Bread Loaf and the Community of Writers. Her poems have been published by *Split This Rock, Poets.org, Anomaly, Narrative*, and others. She lives in Washington, DC, and wants to empower immigrants to tell their own stories.

Jim Minick

Jim Minick is the author or editor of eight books, including *The Intimacy of Spoons* (poetry), *Without Warning: The Tornado of Udall, Kansas* (nonfiction), *Fire Is Your Water*, (novel), and *The Blueberry Years: A Memoir of Farm and Family*. Minick's work has appeared in many publications including *The New York Times, Oxford American, Orion, Shenandoah, Conversations with Wendell Berry, Appalachian Journal, Wind*, and *The Sun*. He serves as Coeditor of *Pine Mountain Sand & Gravel*.

Molly Peacock

Molly Peacock is the author of eight collections of poetry, including *The Widow's Crayon Box, The Analyst: Poems* and *Cornucopia: New and Selected Poems*. Her poems appear in leading literary journals such as *Poetry* and are included in *A Century of Poetry from The New Yorker* and *The Oxford Book of American Poetry*. She is the co-founder of *Poetry in Motion* on New York's subways and buses and the founder of *The Best Canadian Poetry*.

Anna Laura Reeve

Anna Laura Reeve is the author of *Reaching the Shore of the Sea of Fertility* (Belle Point Press, 2023), which was a finalist for the 2023 Weatherford Award in Poetry. She is the winner of the 2022 Adrienne Rich Award for Poetry and the 2024 Emerging Writers Award from the East Tennessee Writers Hall of Fame. Her poems have appeared in *The Adroit Journal, The Cincinnati Review, Beloit Poetry Journal*, and others.

Ron Smith

Ron Smith was poet laureate of Virginia from 2014 to 2016. He is the author of five poetry collections: *Running Again in Hollywood Cemetery, Moon Road, Its Ghostly Workshop, The Humility of the Brutes*, and *That Beauty in the Trees*. Smith currently serves as Consultant in Poetry and Prose at St. Christopher's School in Richmond, Virginia.

B.A. Van Sise

B.A. Van Sise is an author and photographic artist with three monographs: the visual poetry anthology *Children of Grass* with Mary-Louise Parker, *Invited to Life* with Mayim Bialik, and *On the National Language* with DeLanna Studi. He has won the Anthem Award, the Lascaux Prize for Nonfiction, and the Independent Book Publishers Awards gold medal, twice.

Hilde Weisert

Hilde Weisert's 2015 poetry collection *The Scheme of Things* was published by David Robert Books. Her work has appeared in such magazines as *Ms, The Cincinnati Review, The Hudson Review, Plume, Prairie Schooner,* and *The Sun,* and anthologies including *Choice Words: Writers on Abortion* (Haymarket Books, 2020). Awards include the 2017 Gretchen Warren Award (New England Poetry Club), 2016 Tiferet Journal Poetry Award, 2008 Lois Cranston Poetry Prize, and 2009, 2016, 2020 Fellowships from the Virginia Center for the Creative Arts. She lives in Chapel Hill, NC and Sandisfield, MA.

www.ingramcontent.com/pod-product-compliance
Lightning Source LLC
Chambersburg PA
CBHW060356180626
46817CB00008B/3034